Fifty, Furred, and Fabulous!

A Malsum Pass Series Story

Kimberly Forrest

WHO SAYS ROMANCE IS just for twenty-somethings?

With her fiftieth birthday looming, wolf shifter Ginny Weller is finally taking her dream vacation. Sun, surf, and cocktails await. This is her chance to have an adventure... and what better adventure was there than a steamy, no-holds-barred fling with a sexy stranger?

Scott Sloane is living his dream of seeing the world. He stays in a place until his wolf gets antsy and then it's off to a new destination. That all changes when he meets Ginny. For the first time his wolf isn't thinking about moving on, but finally setting down roots. He has seven days to convince her that the best souvenir she can take home from her vacation is him.

For Ginny

CHAPTER ONE

GINNY WELLER GRINNED AT her reflection in the full-length mirror. Her fiftieth birthday may be just around the corner, but she still filled out the strapless bikini she'd chosen just fine. Okay, so her boobs and ass may not be quite as high as they once were, and certain spots may be a bit softer, but she was still going to strut her stuff out on that beach.

Grabbing the floppy coral sun hat that was a perfect match to the new bikini and beautifully complimented her skin tone, Ginny perched it on top of her artfully done messy bun – just the right amount of her thick, golden-brown hair escaping to frame her face and accentuate the long lines of her neck. *Fabulous*. Who said an almost fifty-year-old couldn't rock it?

Next came the sheer cover-up that didn't cover much of anything, but completed the look, and her large sunglasses with the rhinestone hearts that had been a case of love at first sight when she'd spied them on the rack. Letting out a delighted little laugh, she snatched up her cellphone to take a selfie. She'd never been much for that sort of thing, but this look called for photographic evidence. Sending the picture off in a message to her friend and co-worker, Rin, who was currently holding the fort back home in Malsum Pass, Ginny reviewed her mental to-do list.

She loved lists. She lived by lists. Her lists had lists... Shopping lists, client lists, supply lists, and general to-do lists. But today, her list was small and ended with a big *Have Fun!* With that in mind, she grabbed her beach bag, left her room, and walked out of her hotel onto the white sandy beach.

A tropical storm had recently blown through, but today, blue skies stretched as far as the eye could see. Taking a deep breath of salt-tinged air, Ginny marveled at the sights before her. Born and raised in the mountains of Vermont, palm trees were new and exciting, not to mention the rolling waves of blue topped with white foam, lapping at the shore. And the colors... Everything seemed brighter here for some reason. It stole her breath with its postcard perfection.

Toeing off a sandal, Ginny pushed her foot into the soft, warm sand and grinned. Oh yeah, a girl could get used to this. With a delighted chuckle, she shed the other sandal and stuffed both into her bag before making her way to a selection of lounge chairs. That's when she spotted the bar covered in faded palm leaves to give it the look of a tiki hut. It may be early by some people's standards, but she was suddenly craving something with rum, and fruit, with a clever little umbrella. After all, this was supposed to be her adventure of a lifetime, the first real vacation she'd taken in years, and she had every intention of enjoying it to the fullest.

The idea had taken root after talking to some of the females from a visiting pack. Every year they took a cruise to Alaska where they stayed with one of the resident packs for a week of partying, and for the females – mate hunting.

They had made it sound like so much fun, and Ginny had wanted to go so badly she could almost taste it. Unfortunately, as the only accountant in town, she always had so much to do. Her chances of taking more than a long weekend were slim to none. Her conscience wouldn't allow it. Then, fate stepped in and delivered an answer in the form of Rin Hayashi, Kitsune, and a CPA in need of a job.

Hallelujah!

With so many vacation possibilities opening up before her, Ginny had very nearly called and booked that Alaskan getaway – until she thought more about it. Alaska was probably gorgeous, and the available male wolves in the pack might be the most handsome specimens on the planet, but did she want her first real vacation in years to be in a locale that was even colder than Vermont?

Ah, no. Ginny wanted a beach, baby! She needed sun, heat, and the sight of shirtless men all tan and glowing, not more beards and flannel. So, she'd picked up a bunch of brochures – some of them for cruises, others for resorts like this one – carried them with her wherever she went and had studied them almost religiously. The brochure for this place had practically called to her. Her eyes continually returned to it, her fingers finding it without error every time she reached into her bag. It was like the Fates were handing her the answer, and she'd have been a fool not to follow.

"What can I get you, love?"

Ginny nearly giggled at the flirtatious tone of the bartender who was smiling at her and was half tempted to just ask him questions so she could continue to hear him speak in that lyrical accent.

Out of habit, Ginny inhaled, using her keen sense of smell to help her fill in the blanks. The man was human, not surprising in this area, built tall and strong with smooth, dark mahogany skin that appeared even darker next to the pale yellow of his polo shirt emblazoned with the hotel's insignia. The width of his biceps strained the seams of the short sleeves. Nice. The man could hold her attention for more than his speaking voice, that was for sure. But back to the question at hand...

"I have no idea," she exclaimed with a laugh, looking at the list of drinks written on the chalkboard on the back wall. It was the truth. Never having been much of a drinker, she had no idea what was in any of those drinks. "Something fruity, alcoholic, and pretty."

The bartender winked. "I'll fix you right up."

What Ginny walked away with was exactly what she had always pictured – colorful, full of fruit, and topped with an umbrella. Taking a sip through the tiny straw, she nearly gasped at the flavors. If she wasn't careful, she would suck this baby down in two seconds flat and be stumbling across the beach instead of strutting.

Selecting a spot close to the water, Ginny settled into her lounger for a few minutes of people-watching. Lots of oil-slicked, tan skin minimally covered by brightly colored bikinis. If a woman was wearing a one-piece bathing suit on this beach, Ginny couldn't find her. She grinned. *That's right, ladies. Strut your stuff!*

There were men in board shorts, even some speedos, children playing in the surf with their parents while others were building sandcastles, an older gentleman walking his dog…

Another sip of her drink and her eyes went to the water. It looked so inviting, glittering under the bright sunshine.

Standing, Ginny stripped off her cover-up and made her way down to the beckoning waves. There had been some warnings about a strong riptide, but she wasn't going to go far – just enough to get wet and feel the ocean for the first time.

It was an odd sensation, the push, and pull of the waves against her legs, the feel of the wet sand shifting under her feet, but the water was delightfully cool on her heated skin. With water lapping at her hips, she stopped and dug her toes into the bottom for balance. Looking over her shoulder, she admired the beach and the line of palm trees and hotels beyond. That's when she saw him. Standing by a lounger not too far from hers, he was stripping a t-shirt off over his head to expose a tan torso rippling with muscles, above a pair of bright white board shorts that had what looked like a black dragon on one side. Her mouth went dry and it felt like her brain was about to short-circuit. *Good golly, Miss Molly, that man was fine.*

As if sensing the intensity of her stare, his head snapped in her direction and she could practically feel his eyes pinning her to the spot. She couldn't help it, she struck a pose. With a hand on her hip, her back arched just a bit, and her chin lifted a notch. *That's right, look at me, big handsome.* And he was, too... Unfortunately, those fickle Fates decided to ruin her allure as it sent a wave crashing up and over her head knocking her completely off her feet.

Coughing and sputtering, Ginny lurched upright and pushed sodden clumps of hair from her face. She'd lost her hat, and her sunglasses, but it wasn't until she looked down to try to find those two items that she discovered the naughty wave had also taken off with her bikini top.

Chapter Two

Ginny was still gasping and trying not to gag over the burn of saltwater that had gone up her nose, down her throat, and, by the feel of it, into her lungs. She was clutching an arm over her naked boobs when a very tan and muscular chest was suddenly in her face.

"I've got you," she heard a deep voice drawl before a t-shirt – which she would bet smelled fantastic if she could've smelled anything at the moment – was pulled over her head. The soft cotton was still warm from his body and clung instantly to her wet skin but at least it returned her modesty. She may be a shifter, but public nudity had never been her thing.

Looking up to thank her knight in shining armor, Ginny was once again struck by the man who had so fascinated her moments before her tumble. Dark, neatly trimmed hair just touched with silver that sparkled in the sun near his temples, a shadow of whiskers on his strong, square jaw that held a fair bit of silver as well, and dark eyes full of concern. That concern triggered the mortifying reminder that he had witnessed that graceless display.

"Are you okay? Are you hurt?"

Such a great voice – smooth, deep, and sexy with a hint of underlying command. An alpha male. Yummy. Ginny shivered, not the least bit cold, yet her hero took it that way as he wrapped a strong arm around her shoulders and ushered her out of the water. "Come on, let's get you dry."

No chance of that, Ginny thought with a devilish mental smirk. Not when those big strong arms were around her, holding her close. She let him lead her back to her lounger. Under the guise of needing extra help with her balance, Ginny slung her arm around his back and let her fingers trail over his upper arm before she gave the bicep a little squeeze. Ooh, he was strong, the muscles rock hard under her hand. Nice. With regret, she released him once they were back to her lounger and collapsed rather awkwardly into her seat. Picking up her drink, she didn't even bother with the straw as she gulped the fruity concoction down in hopes of ridding herself of the aftertaste from swallowing half the ocean.

"I'll go grab you a bottle of water," her hero said before taking off. She watched him go, unable to tear her eyes off that taut backside. Until she realized her nose was leaking. Quickly snatching up her bag, she rummaged through it to find tissues. She found her discarded sandals, a brush – useful, but not what she needed at the moment – her wallet, cell phone, sunblock, gum, compact, lip balm… aha! Tissues. Finally. Pulling one of the small squares free of the plastic, she gave her nose a hearty blow, grateful her hero wasn't close enough to hear the inelegant goose honk. Stuffing the used tissue into her bag, Ginny pulled out her compact to make sure she didn't have anything unsightly left behind on her face and let out a screech. She had seaweed in her hair! Her hero had seen her like this? And after she'd already embarrassed herself by going ass over teakettle in the surf. *Perfect. Way to nail that first impression.* Quickly disengaging the slimy green rope, she threw it down in disgust, only to spot her very apparent nipples through the white t-shirt now clinging wetly to her chest. It looked like she'd just entered a wet t-shirt contest. Scrabbling for her towel, she whipped it around her torso. Slightly mollified, Ginny inhaled once and then again just to be sure. Now that her nose was clear, she picked up the scent that still clung to his shirt. Laundry soap, warm sunshine mixed with salt water, and a masculine scent that was probably either his soap or his deodorant, but none of those were what had her eyes widening in disbelief. Nope. What now had her mouth hanging open as she gawked in amazement at her savior as he approached – instead of situating herself elegantly on the lounger – was the unmistakable scent of a fellow wolf shifter. What were the odds?

As soon as he reached her side, he handed her a bottle, cold and wet with condensation, and Ginny gratefully cracked the top as he settled into the sand next to her. "I picked up your scent almost immediately and was planning to come over and introduce myself." Thrusting out a hand, her hero grinned. "Scott Sloane, Wyoming pack."

Drying off her damp hand on an edge of her towel, she gripped his much larger, calloused palm. "Ginny Weller, Vermont."

Scott let out a low whistle. "I didn't realize any packs were still around in Vermont."

"Just us. We're small, but still kicking," she told him with a smile. "Thank you for helping me out." Grimacing, she added, "The wave took me by surprise."

And took her top, and her hat, *and* her favorite sunglasses. Honestly, she was more upset about the latter. She loved those sunglasses and they looked so good on her face. Her spare pair wasn't nearly as flattering.

"My good deed for the day," Scott was saying. "So what brings you here, Ginny Weller from Vermont?"

Ginny settled deeper into her lounge chair and took another drink from the water bottle. "A much-needed vacation. You?"

"I live here at the moment."

The statement was surprising. Shifters rarely drifted far from their pack, and if they did, it was usually to join with another. A lone wolf was a rarity, for they had strength in numbers.

"After I retired from the military, I decided to travel and see parts of the world that weren't all torn up. When I find a place I like, I stick around for a while."

Ginny took a closer look at the male. Yes, he had silver threading through his hair, but he looked far too young to be retired.

"How long were you in the military?"

Scott leaned back on an elbow in the sand. "Twenty-two years," he said with a sigh. "Been out seven now, and seen a lot of beautiful places in this world. Never been to Vermont though. I may have to add that to my list," he added with a wink and a smile.

A male with a list... she loved lists. Ginny didn't even realize how vigorously she was nodding. "Oh, you should."

Scott grinned. "Are you here with your pack, Ginny? Your mate?"

Before she thought about the possible dangers of letting a veritable stranger know that she was traveling alone, she had already shaken her head no.

Her hero's grin got even wider, displaying laugh lines and an adorable dimple. This was a man who looked like he smiled easily and a lot. She liked that. A decidedly interested spark made his eyes twinkle with appreciation and Ginny's belly clenched as her blood heated in her veins.

"Well, then I'd consider it an honor to show you the best spots in the area. How about we start with some dinner and dancing tonight?"

Throwing caution to the wind, Ginny accepted.

Chapter Three

Scott had to pry his eyes away from Ginny and focus on acting casual, keeping his voice neutral before he scared the woman away. Christ, when she admitted she didn't have a mate, his wolf had practically lunged inside his skin with the need to immediately claim her, drag her off somewhere to mark her as his, and never let her go. He was forty-seven years old, far from virginal or celibate, and yet no woman – shifter or human – had ever affected him so viscerally. This one left him feeling positively primal. It was crazy. *He* was crazy. He'd just met her.

He'd picked up her scent immediately on the breeze and as he'd told her, had intended to come over and introduce himself. Wolf shifters on the island were a rarity. Those that did come for a vacation were usually in a pack and typically twenty-somethings cutting loose on break from college. Not this woman. He could see at a glance that she was older – definitely not too young for him which had immediately piqued his interest – but when that wave had taken her bikini top… his eyes had about popped out of his head and his other head south of the border had immediately stood up and saluted. The woman had a great set of tits.

He had bolted across the sand and into the water without hesitation, eager to play her knight in shining armor. It had hit him then, the insane realization that if anyone else had gotten there before him, he would have fought them for the right to cover her with *his* T-shirt, to be the one she looked up at with those gorgeous eyes filled with appreciation. See? Crazy. Maybe he'd been out in the sun too long? No. The tropical clime of the island was child's play compared to humping it out in desert heat in full gear. He was fully aware of exactly what this was, or rather, what practically every wolf shifter on the planet would say. The mating bond. It was said to be some extra sense that shifters possessed where they could sense their soul mate when they were near. He'd never believed in it before, thought it was just a healthy case of attraction paired with a large dose of lust that his people had romanticized into something magical to explain why some males immediately lost their heads over a particular female. Now he wasn't so sure as he tried and failed to regain some control. His brain was telling him to pull back, retreat before he was in too deep, but his wolf was howling to get closer.

Ginny Weller from Vermont felt big. She felt special. Most of all, she felt like his, and in all his years, he'd never felt anything even close to this level of attraction. Dinner and dancing were a good start, but if he had his way, it would only be the beginning.

Clearing his throat to make sure the possessive growl that was rumbling dangerously close to the surface stayed buried, Scott asked the question that had been burning in his brain and held his breath as he waited for her answer. "So, how long are you here, Ginny?"

"A week," she replied with a smile, and his wolf howled in protest.

One week. Seven days to make a lasting impression and that was only if she allowed him to spend each of those days with her. If he screwed this up, she could be telling him to get lost before he even had a chance to take her out to dinner. So he couldn't screw this up. One week. High stakes. He needed a battle plan. This time, the growl he swallowed down was one laced with pure determination.

A date! She had a date. A makeover hadn't been on her to-do list, but when she'd gone back to the hotel room to look through the assortment of clothes she'd packed, she'd been dissatisfied with the offerings. She hadn't been on a date in ages and Scott Sloane was hot, hot, hot. If she was going to do this, she was going to do it right. She didn't just want to look good, she wanted to look amazing.

"You look fabulous!"

That worked too.

Standing before a mirror in the little boutique, Ginny grinned at the woman just behind her in the reflection. She wanted to twirl, and the dress she'd decided on was perfect for just that sort of movement. Rose in color, it was comprised of light gauzy layers cinched tight at the waist to flow into a skirt that would flutter in the breeze and lift enticingly high should her dance partner spin her. With a halter neck that left her back bare, it made her feel sexy, and ultra-feminine, and was exactly the type of dress one was meant to dance in.

She had thought to wear her hair down in beachy waves, but the stylist had talked her out of it. "That neckline you've chosen screams up-do." And Ginny had to admit, the woman was right. The twist she'd ended up with was soft, a few curling tendrils left loose to caress her neck and shoulders and completed the look of sexy femininity. Her belly fluttered with giddy anticipation. She couldn't wait for Scott to see her.

"No man will be able to resist you tonight," her stylist told her with a pleased smile.

Ginny was only concerned with one man, and when she spotted him waiting for her in the hotel lobby right at the agreed-upon time, she could barely resist the joyous laughter that bubbled up from deep inside. The look on his face was pure awe and the gaze exploring her form glittered with admiration. She couldn't have asked for a better reaction.

Wasting no time, he approached and took her hand, the warm strength of his fingers sending a current of awareness shooting up her arm that made her toes want to curl. "You look amazing."

"So do you," she said with a smile and it was the truth. Black dress pants, perfectly pressed, hugged that tight backside and those narrow hips. The gray dress shirt he'd donned was also perfectly pressed, the creases sharp down the sleeves. He'd forgone a tie and left the throat open in deference to the heat – or perhaps he wasn't much of a tie person – but that triangle of tanned skin just below his neck held her attention for several hard beats of her heart. Earlier today she'd seen him in nothing but a pair of shorts, yet here she was gawking at his neck practically dry-mouthed at that tiny hint of flesh. She wanted to lick it, nibble on it...

"Are you ready?"

Hell yeah, she was. Ready and willing. It had been way too long since she'd been intimate with a man and her body was reminding her of that with a low throb of desire, her blood practically humming in her veins. She had to restrain the urge to drag him back to her room and have her wicked way with him. But he meant was she ready to leave. Ginny swallowed hard to keep from growling and nodded. Her voice was a bit gruff when she asked, "Where are we going?"

"A little place mostly frequented by the locals. I think you're going to love it."

And she did. Absolutely. Once she'd gotten her libido back under control and wasn't in danger of dragging Scott off and jumping his bones. Off the beaten path so to speak, the little place was lit by torches outside and colorful lanterns inside, while the atmosphere was alive with the sound of music and laughter. The scents coming from the kitchen were enough to make her mouth water and set her belly to rumbling.

Scott must have been a regular since they were greeted with joyful shouts of "Sarge!" as soon as they walked through the door.

Glancing up at him with a smile, Ginny raised a brow. "You were a sergeant?"

Scott shot her a lopsided grin that she found completely adorable since it unleashed that dimple. "Yes, ma'am," he drawled. "Sergeant First Class Sloane, at your service."

"You brought a woman," was said just behind Ginny and had her turning around to look at the speaker. The woman was only about five feet tall, dark-skinned and plump, and adorned with seemingly every color of the rainbow from the scarves around her black riot of curls to the skirt that ended at her sandaled feet. She was looking Ginny over with a wide, friendly grin before turning a pursed-lip look of consideration to Scott. "She's too pretty for a scoundrel like you."

Scott threw his head back and laughed before leaning down and embracing the woman in a hard hug. "She is, Mother," he concurred, "but she took pity on this poor country boy and agreed to be seen with me."

The woman gave Scott's back a few hard claps before she broke away to once more address Ginny. "You don't be believing a word that comes out of this boy's mouth," she warned in the lyrical accent of the island. Snorting, she shook her head. "Poor country boy, my foot."

Scott let out another good-natured chuckle before his strong, slightly calloused hand landed on the bare skin of Ginny's back, the feeling making her shiver with awareness, and shot her too-long ignored libido back to hopping. "Ginny, this is Alvita."

Ginny put her hand out with a smile, but instead of shaking it, Alvita gripped the hand in both of hers. "You'll call me Mother, just like everyone else." Then with a sharp nod, Alvita released her hand and turned away with a gesture for them to follow. "Come. Sit. Eat."

Alvita wasn't the only one who came over to see Scott as huge quantities of food were set on the table before her, steaming and aromatic. Good-natured ribbing abounded as curious eyes took in Ginny before they nodded at Scott in approval.

"They like you." Scott grinned over the rim of his glass before taking a sip. "I knew they would."

Pleased, Ginny returned the smile and looked around the little restaurant once more. "I like them, too. Everyone is so friendly."

Setting his glass down, Scott slid his hand across the table and Ginny took it, allowing him to interlace his fingers with hers. They'd just met, and yet, it felt so natural, so right...

"So, Ginny Weller from Vermont. Care to take pity once again on this poor country boy and be seen dancing with me?"

Nodding, Ginny stood with anticipation. There was no set dance floor, they just blended in with the others that were openly dancing in any space they could find. Their bodies moved together beautifully, as if they'd been made to fit together, fluid and swaying, pressed tight as they moved to the rhythm. Scott's hand was firm on her back, the fingers of his other hand still entwined with hers. The way they danced was in no way provocative, yet the feeling was sensual, nearly erotic, with the music only seeming to heighten her already elevated senses. It seemed the most natural thing in the world to press her lips to that little V of golden skin just below his throat.

She heard his low growl of approval and felt her nipples tighten and a low clench of need in her womb. His fingers skimmed up her spine to the nape of her neck and goosebumps rose on her skin, as well as a delightful shiver of arousal. She leaned deeper into his embrace, reveling in a connection she hadn't felt in years.

It didn't matter that she had just met the male today, she felt it with every beat of her heart, her wolf practically howling in her brain with the knowledge that she was exactly where she was supposed to be.

Chapter Four

"How is someone as smart and beautiful as you not mated? Are all the males in Vermont blind?" Scott asked as they shared one of Alvita's homemade desserts.

Having congratulated herself on not dragging Scott off the dance-floor and straight back to her hotel to rip his clothes off, Ginny was in too good a mood – possibly due to the atmosphere, and definitely because of the company – to feel the wash of sorrow that usually accompanied thoughts of her deceased mate. Swallowing the bite of dessert, she took a sip of her drink before replying. "I was mated. He passed away several years ago. A problem with his heart that no one knew about."

Scott's hand once again moved across the table to twine with hers. "I'm sorry for your loss."

Ginny nodded, her lips turning up in a small smile tinged with sadness. "Jimmy had a good life." Shaking her head, she grinned in remembrance. *Such a life he'd lived*. "He was wild. An adrenaline junky. Always pushing boundaries, riding the edge, looking for his next thrill. He used to say to me, 'You're not here for a long time, Ginger Snaps, you're here for a good time'."

The familiar saying brought on a rush of memory. All of Jimmy's adventures: skydiving, whitewater rafting, snowboarding... He always used to invite her to go with him and in the early years of their marriage, she'd happily tagged along with him and his adrenaline junky buddies. Later, however, there was always something to do – something on her list that needed to be checked off. *Next time*, she'd tell him, *next time for sure*. And then one day, there were no more chances to keep her promise. No more next time. James Weller was gone. Clearing her throat to dislodge the lump of emotion, Ginny took another drink. "So, he may have been taken early, but he lived a lifetime of adventure." It was her life that looked rather sad by comparison, and something she was finally getting a chance to rectify.

Needing to change the subject before her mood spiraled so low there'd be no chance of recovery, Ginny brought the subject around to her dinner companion. "And you? How is it you're not mated?"

She probably should have asked him if he was mated before she'd agreed to this date. She'd just assumed he wasn't, which, in hindsight, was spectacularly stupid. If he told her now that he had a mate stashed somewhere, she was going to bite him, and not in a good way...

He shrugged. "Just never found the right female."

She could work with that. She had promised herself that these seven days of vacation would be chock-full of adventure before she ushered in the big five-oh, and a passionate, no-strings-attached tryst with a sexy stranger was sounding like just the thing. Her sex-deprived body was certainly on board. It was something she would never do back home, and therefore, absolutely perfect. She was a mature, sophisticated, unattached female after all, perfectly capable of enjoying an affair. Before she could change her mind and possibly chicken out, she opened her mouth, the invitation rolling off her tongue. "Do you want to come back to my hotel with me?"

Scott didn't even hesitate before he stood, pulled some money out to leave on the table, and took her hand. They practically ran for the door and Ginny suddenly felt like a teenager again, all over-active hormones and the thrill of the chase.

The ride back to the hotel was a blur of sensation. Scott drove with one hand on the steering wheel while the other cupped the nape of her neck. His thumb softly stroked her jawline and the sensitive skin of her throat, making goosebumps rise, while Ginny's fingers were busy undoing several buttons of his shirt to reach the heated flesh beneath. Her hands skimmed over strong muscles and the thin mat of hair on his chest, the sensation making her fingertips tingle.

The vehicle had barely come to a complete stop in the parking lot before she was leaning over and pulling his mouth to hers. She was so hungry. So unbelievably parched for his kisses. And Scott Sloane gave back one hell of a kiss. His teeth nipped at her bottom lip before his tongue invaded hungrily, the only sound in the car was their heavy breathing and a growl of need – hers or his? It didn't matter.

Scott broke the kiss with a shuddering breath as he leaned his forehead against hers, his grip strong on the back of her neck but not so hard it hurt. "Are you sure?"

"I've never been more sure of anything in my life," Ginny told him with conviction. She ached with wanting him. Her body was attuned to his in a way that defied explanation.

Within moments he was out of the car and opening her door to scoop her up into his arms. "You won't regret this," he growled against her lips as his mouth once more took control of hers.

Ginny barely noticed the lobby of the hotel or the elevator ride up to her room, her attention solely on Scott and the way he made her feel. He released her only long enough for her to retrieve the key card to let them into the cool, currently dark space that would be her home for the week and then he was kissing her again, devouring her, and thrilling her down to her toes.

Never breaking that heated kiss, Scott lowered her to the soft bed and followed her down, his welcome weight settling between her thighs. The feeling of all of that male heat against her only served to notch up her already desperate desire. Groaning as she felt the neck of the halter dress loosen, Ginny arched upward, begging for his touch on her aching breasts. Scott immediately obliged, his mouth hot against the tight bud of her nipple, while his palm stroked and squeezed the other breast by turns.

She moaned deep in her throat, her hips lifting off the mattress to grind against the hard ridge of his erection pressed deliciously against her core. The clothes between them were a nuisance and one she wanted to be rid of, so her grip may have been a bit too hard as she tore at Scott's shirt and sent buttons flying to ping against the headboard and nightstand.

Scott growled his approval, pushing himself away from her breasts only long enough to shed the shirt before he returned, his teeth scraping over one sensitive peak and then the other while his big hand cupped the outside of her thigh and slid upward until he was gripping her hip. Holding her in place, he kissed his way down her sternum, over the bunched fabric at her waist, to the apex of her thighs.

Ginny's head thrashed on the pillow as he nuzzled her through her panties with his nose. "You are so beautiful," she heard him utter before his fingers moved that strip of silk to one side and his tongue touched that swollen bundle of nerves that was crying for his attention. She nearly screamed, it felt so incredible. She was a bowstring stretched taut, ready to snap at any moment.

His lips pressed closer as he sucked and licked at the core of her desire, but it was the finger he slid inside of her that was Ginny's undoing. The scream that had been locked in her throat broke free as the intensity of her climax washed over her in wave after wave of pleasure.

Replete, Ginny collapsed back against the mattress. She hadn't even been aware she'd risen her upper body until her head reconnected with the softness of the pillow. Her breath left her in short staccato pants, while her fingers, which had been tightly gripped in Scott's hair, relaxed their hold and stroked over his scalp.

He placed a gentle kiss on the inside of one thigh and then the other. Climbing back up over her body, he held himself above her with strong arms and leaned down to kiss her softly on the lips. "You're not going to fall asleep on me, are you, Ginny Weller?" Scott teased, nuzzling her cheek.

Her eyelids were feeling pretty heavy, but no way was she going to miss even a moment of this. Grinning, Ginny slid her hand down and gripped the rigid length pushing against the front of his pants. "Not a chance."

With a beautiful smile, Scott once more sealed his lips to hers while Ginny's fingers worked at releasing what promised to be an impressive erection. As soon as it was free, jutting proudly from his hips in an invitation she couldn't ignore, Ginny wrapped her fingers around the hard, hot length and stroked. Raising her hips, she slid that blunt head against the swollen, wet folds at her center and hissed out a breath at the feeling while Scott groaned loudly, the sound filling the room.

"You're so hot," he growled. "So wet. I want in." Dipping his head, he dropped a kiss on her lips with another groan. "But I want us both naked." Sitting up, he made quick work of both of their remaining clothes before grabbing a foil packet from his wallet and quickly sheathing his erection.

Settling his weight once more between her legs, Ginny writhed against him impatiently, eager to feel him inside of her. She felt so empty. She needed this. Needed him. Her hands gripped almost frantically at his hard-muscled shoulders and tried to pull him down. But Scott was in no hurry, despite the iron-hard evidence of his arousal. He slid his nose over her cheek in a nuzzling caress, dropped gentle, sucking kisses on her throat, and licked enticingly over her collarbone while a low, rumbling growl vibrated through his chest.

The sound was so sexy Ginny nearly came again.

"Please," she breathed.

"You're sure?"

Eventually, when she once again had full control of her faculties, she'd probably think back and appreciate the care and concern his question showed, but right now, she was greedy and impatient. With a growl that was almost savage in intensity, she lunged, her teeth latching onto his shoulder. The bite wasn't hard enough to break his skin, but it got the point across.

With a low, sexy laugh, and a murmured, "Impatient. I like that," Scott slid home, his erection filling her, stretching her so perfectly that Ginny cried out with pleasure. And then he began to move. Every thrust brought her closer to that sought-after pinnacle, building, and building until she thought for sure every muscle in her body was going to snap from being stretched so tight.

Scott's breath was a hot rush against her neck as he murmured little words of encouragement, and told her how beautiful she was... then one of his hands slid between them, his thumb making contact with that swollen bundle of nerves, and Ginny was crashing over the edge, the world seeming to shatter around her in brilliant points of light and color.

She heard a snarl as Scott's thrusts became harder. A nearly primal growl, and then the throbbing pulse of his length inside her still-quivering body as he followed her over the edge with a shout of completion.

She'd provoked that sexy reaction. Ginny smiled in rather smug satisfaction as she held her lover's heated body close.

Scott should have been sleeping. He should have passed out cold after the incredible, mind-blowing pleasures he'd just experienced with this woman. But instead of snoring away in dreamland, he was too busy staring at the sleeping form cuddled tight to his side. His mate. He'd felt the connection, the knowledge that she was special to him when he'd first met her but now it felt even bigger. In less than a day, Ginny Weller had become the center of his universe, and finding sleep after such a monumental realization was nearly impossible.

They'd been right. All those stories about the mating bond that he'd so casually brushed off as nonsense, had been true. He got it now. He felt it.

He had to suppress the urge to wake her just so that he could once more see that beautiful smile light up her face, hear the lilt of her voice that called to his inner wolf like no one before her, and feel her fingers on his skin. Scott blew out a hard breath. Patience. She needed her sleep, he reminded himself firmly. What kind of male would he be to deny his female the rest she needed?

Did she feel it too? Having not put much stock in the stories, he'd never paid attention to whether it was a two-way street. What if it wasn't the same for her? His first, second, and even third inclination was to immediately wake her up and ask her. He fisted his hand. Was he insane? If she didn't feel the same, he would be shooting himself in the foot. Better to keep his mouth shut and see where things led.

She'd already had a mate and lost him. She may very well never want to tie herself to anyone again. The thought caused his chest to tighten as the air locked in his lungs.

He couldn't just claim her and keep her, she needed to claim him too. But would she? His eyes flicked to her suitcase on the other side of the room. Six days left. He had six days to get her to decide that he was worth keeping. Worth taking home with her to Vermont...

For the first time in years, Scott Sloane was considering setting down roots somewhere and Ginny Weller was the cause.

Chapter Five

Ginny fell asleep in Scott's arms and woke to breakfast in bed. She could certainly get used to this. Her lips – slightly puffy from all the kissing the night before – seemed permanently glued into a smile. The sunshine streaming in through the windows seemed brighter, and she felt downright bubbly. Amazing what a night of great sex could do.

"What would you like to do today?" Scott asked as he popped a chunk of pineapple into his mouth and settled next to her on the bed.

Have more great sex... That was the first thought that popped into her head, especially with Scott sitting so close to her, smelling so incredibly good, and looking so scrumptious without a shirt on. But she only had six days left and she was still determined to pack this vacation with as many adventures as possible.

Giving it some thought, she chewed her bite of banana muffin. So many options. It was one of the reasons this particular resort had held so much appeal. "Snorkeling?"

Scott nodded. "Snorkeling it is," he said, dropping a kiss on the side of her throat. "I know a great spot."

They'd had to drive some ways to reach their destination, but Ginny was thrilled. The water in the little inlet was calm, crystal clear, not too deep, and surrounded by rocks that were perfect for sitting on and relaxing should they have the urge.

"The fish here will come right up to you," Scott promised as he helped her tighten the strap on her mask. "And if you like this, and want to see more, later we can go out on a boat and check out the reef not too far from here."

Excited by the prospect, Ginny put the snorkel in her mouth and bent down to stick her face in the water. So clear! And Scott had been correct. The fish that swam past her, even up to her, were tiny yet colorful and had absolutely no fear of the two shifters that had invaded their domain.

Turning her face to look at Scott who was floating right next to her, she grinned, not caring that she probably looked ridiculous trying to smile around the plastic tube in her mouth. Scott gave her a thumbs-up and then laced his fingers with hers as they floated through the calm waters. Idyllic, perfect, better than she could ever have imagined. Ginny looked around in awe. She could see so far out. Whenever she'd gone snorkeling in one of the lakes back home, the water had always been a murky green where she could barely see even a foot in front of her. Not the case here.

They had been in the water for maybe fifteen minutes, perhaps a bit longer when a tiny fish – barely the size of her palm – decided to check her out more closely. The little thing was quite curious, and nearly giggling with delight at the way he darted around her, Ginny stuck her free hand out toward the fish.

Ouch! Rearing back with a muffled screech, Ginny planted her feet firmly on the ocean floor and stood up, wrenching her hand away from Scott and gripping her now-smarting wrist as she spat the snorkel out of her mouth.

Scott was immediately beside her. "What happened?"

"It bit me!"

Feeling little bumps and nudges around her ankles and knees that only unsettled her further, Ginny wrenched off the mask, made for one of the rocks, and hauled herself post-haste out of the water, mumbling the entire time, "Stupid little piranha must not have been satisfied with the food in the Amazon and had to come here to ruin my day."

"Let me see," Scott said gently as he pulled her hand away from her wrist. The injury was tiny, and examining it, Ginny felt a bit foolish now for making such a big deal out of it. Two little crescents of blood barely even as big as the tip of her pinky nail marred the inside of her wrist just below the heel of her hand. Bending forward, he kissed the tiny wound, his eyes lifting to hers with such heat in his gaze that Ginny's breath caught. Okay, maybe making a big deal of it wasn't a bad thing...

"That fish has excellent taste," Scott told her with a smile that was positively wicked and made her belly clench. "I want to nibble on you too."

Oh, yes, please.

"Better?"

Her mouth dry, Ginny could only nod as Scott's tongue flicked against the tiny pulse beat on her wrist and slowly worked his way up her arm. "Anywhere else you need me to kiss?" he asked, his voice lowering to a seductive growl.

All thoughts of piranha and other killer fish completely fled her brain as Ginny slid back down into the water and wrapped her free hand around Scott's neck to pull him in for a kiss. Against his lips she teased, "So many, it may take you all day."

His answering growl was much louder this time as he wrapped his arms fully around her and sealed his lips to hers. His hands slid down to her backside and with a slight lift, Ginny wrapped her legs around his waist as he carried her to shore and laid her down on the soft sand. "Another advantage of this particular spot," he groaned against her mouth. "Privacy."

Surrounded by palm trees and rocks, with Scott's vehicle blocking the path, it was easy to pretend that they were alone on a deserted island, with no one to see them shed their swimsuits. No one to witness the complete lack of inhibition as Ginny pushed Scott down her body, demanding he kiss her where she was truly aching, and no one to hear the resulting moans and cries of pleasure he wrung from her as he swiftly brought her to a heart-pounding release.

It was later as they lay in the sand, their bodies still bared to the sun, and their heartbeats finally returned to normal, that Ginny chuckled. "I don't think I'm meant to be in the water."

Scott's fingers never stopped their caressing strokes on her shoulder and upper arm as he lifted his head to look at her with a slight frown. "Why is that?"

"First a wave knocks me over and steals my stuff, and now a fish tried to eat me."

Dropping his head back to the sand with a laugh, Scott's arm tightened around her and pulled until she was lying fully on top of him. His hand furrowed into her hair to release the clip and smooth the thick, damp mass down her back as he gave her a quick peck on the lips. "Plenty of stuff to do inland if you prefer."

"I think I better before things escalate and I end up drowning or being eaten by a shark."

Scott's mouth quirked up in an amused grin. "Whatever your heart desires, my queen. I am but your humble servant."

Ginny wiggled her eyebrows. "Ready to service me?"

His hips lifted beneath her and she felt the proof of just how ready he was once more. Letting out a trill of delighted laughter, Ginny whispered, "My hero," before she lowered her lips to his.

Chapter Six

Ginny was still humming and bobbing her head to the music from last night's festival on the beach. Such a good time. The beach had been lit with what seemed like hundreds of torches, a stage set up for the local musicians, while numerous huts had appeared as if by magic for vendors to hawk their wares. She and Scott had danced on the sand, they'd eaten amazing food, and they'd laughed. So much laughter. He'd shared stories of growing up on a ranch in Wyoming which she may not have heard in its entirety once the picture of him in a cowboy hat and chaps – *only* a cowboy hat and chaps – had thoroughly distracted her, conjuring fantasies she'd love to one day see fulfilled. He'd also told her about his time in the military, several of the stories leaving her gasping for breath with tears streaming down her face she had laughed so hard. And he told her of his dream to see the world and experience as many cultures as he could.

Later, they'd come back to her hotel room, and the way he'd held her, loved her... That's what it had felt like. Love and Ginny had to caution herself not to fall. Had to continually remind herself that this was temporary. Something to enjoy now and think back on fondly later. This wasn't permanent. But she could already feel it. Scott had become important to her. He was more than a fling over a vacation, and she wondered how she was ever going to leave him. Knowing that things would eventually end – would have to end – had added a touch of desperation to every touch, every kiss, every embrace. Maybe she was mistaken, but she was pretty sure she wasn't the only one feeling it. But that was a hope she didn't dare examine any closer in fear it would spoil what time they had left.

This morning, Scott had woken her with a promise of an adventure he was sure she would love. An adventure he had kept secret despite her best efforts to get him to spill. Now that they'd arrived at their destination, however, and Ginny stared up at the sheer cliff face before her, she wasn't sure if the tightness that had taken root in her chest could be called love. Panic? Maybe. Fear? Possibly. That was a really, *really* high climb.

They weren't the only ones here and she did her best to conceal her nerves as several smiling faces greeted her and Scott. Most of the people were already wearing harnesses, helmets, and gloves, but Ginny marveled as she watched one teenage boy, only in a pair of shorts and a sleeveless T-shirt, scramble barefoot up the face of what should be an impossible climb as if it was no big deal. Was the kid part mountain goat?

"Are you ready for an adventure?" Scott asked with a grin as he pulled a bag of equipment she hadn't noticed before from the back of his vehicle.

Ginny swallowed hard, her eyes returning nervously to that cliff. "I've never climbed anything like this before." Not a total lie. She had attempted to climb the cliffs at White Rocks with some others from Malsum Pass back when she was twelve but she hadn't made it very far before she'd hurt her wrist and had to turn back. She'd also done some rock climbing with Jimmy in high school, but nothing of this magnitude – and her high school years had been a long time ago...

"I'll be right beside you every step of the way."

Taking a deep breath, she reminded herself that she was here for an adventure. Her big pre-fiftieth hoorah. Her chance to do all the things she'd missed out on while burying herself in work. With that thought in mind, Ginny stiffened her spine and did some neck rolls and shoulder stretches while she mentally psyched herself up. She could do this. She *would* do this.

Scott stepped in close, cupped her cheek, and kissed her. "I promise you'll love it. Trust me?"

Ginny nodded. She did trust him. Despite their short acquaintance, both she and her inner wolf somehow knew that Scott would never do anything to endanger her. So to keep her mind from freaking out, she studiously avoided looking in the direction of that intimidating cliff while Scott strapped her into a harness and prepared her for the climb.

Honestly, it wasn't as bad as she had first assumed. The hand and footholds were plentiful and not spaced too far apart, and while from a distance, the climb had looked completely vertical, the angle wasn't as steep as it had originally appeared. It also wasn't a race to the top. They climbed leisurely, and as promised, Scott was right beside her the entire way, making sure she wasn't in danger of slipping.

The view that greeted her when she reached the top was worth the jellylike consistency of her arms and the ache deep in her thighs. From this vantage point, she could see the entire island spread out before her, the crystal clear waters beyond, the ships anchored just offshore. Magnificent.

Jimmy would have loved this. That thought was quickly followed by another. Would he be upset that she was having this adventure with someone else? No. She quickly banished the very idea. Not James Weller. That wasn't his style. If there was a heaven, then she knew he was up there looking down at her right now and saying something along the lines of, "Well, it's about damn time!" while he cheered her on. She could almost see the proud grin he would have given her, and hear his voice saying, "Atta girl!" as he pumped his fist in the air.

With her own proud smile, Ginny gripped Scott's hand and laced their fingers together as she took everything in. Inhaling deeply, she marveled. Look at what she'd done. Look at what she had achieved. Filled with a sense of accomplishment, she closed her eyes, threw her head back, and let out an exultant shout, which Scott, as well as several other climbers, quickly joined in on, until the sound was near deafening.

With a grin, Ginny grabbed Scott in a hard hug. "Thank you for this," she whispered, tears of joy filling her eyes. "Thank you so much."

Scott's return squeeze lifted her off her feet and she let out a happy squeal. "My pleasure," he murmured against her forehead. "And thank you for coming into my life, Ginny Weller."

Scott knew he would never forget this moment. The look of excitement and wonder on her face – the pride and exultation – damn he loved this woman. It was also the moment that he decided that if she didn't ask him to come home with her, he'd follow her anyway. He'd follow her to the ends of the earth if that was what it took. He was hers. Heart, mind, body, and soul. He belonged to her.

There at the top of the cliff, they ate a leisurely lunch, chatted with other climbers, and watched the boats moving in the distant waters. They also waved at a few helicopters flying over their heads giving aerial tours of the island.

When it was time to head back down, Scott introduced Ginny to a new love: Rappelling. She laughed and screamed merrily the entire way down, never once fearing that she might fall, filling his chest near to bursting with adoration. And once their feet were solidly on the ground, Scott pulled her into his arms, congratulated her, and just barely bit back the words of love that wanted to tumble off his tongue. *Not yet.* While it all felt so incredibly right it was fragile yet, precious. He wouldn't jeopardize this amazing thing he'd found by rushing.

"Can't move," Ginny groaned, her complaint muffled into the pillows the next morning. The entire rest of the day yesterday she'd crowed to anyone who would listen about her adventure, swearing up and down that it was her best day ever. Look at her now.

She heard Scott chuckle and growled. Bastard. How could he possibly be up and walking around like nothing out of the ordinary had happened when she felt like she'd been run over by a bus – multiple times?

"I thought you wanted to go mountain biking today."

Insanity. Yes, that was the only excuse. She had to have been insane to think she could climb a cliff yesterday and still feel good enough to pop out of bed the next morning to go on a bike tour. Who did she think she was kidding? She was days away from turning fifty, not twenty! "I'm not moving," she grumbled.

Another chuckle had her throwing a pillow at Scott and then hissing when her arm muscles screamed in protest.

"Come on, sweetheart. I've got just the thing to make you feel better."

Ginny snorted. His *thing* wasn't getting anywhere near her. Not when she felt this sore and she told him so – which of course set him to laughing so hard that he collapsed on the bed beside her, shaking the mattress and pulling another groan from her.

"I wasn't suggesting that," he managed to gasp out between chuckles.

Intrigued, Ginny raised a brow only to grimace. How was it possible that even her eyebrows hurt? "If it involves getting out of bed, then I'm not interested."

"I'll carry you. How about that?"

When she didn't answer right away, he cajoled, "Do you really want to waste an entire day in bed when I can guarantee you'll be feeling better in an hour?"

Last night they'd returned to Alvita's, and after sucking down a rather potent margarita, she'd told Scott all about her regrets and her plan to rectify them by filling this vacation with all the adventures she had previously passed up. So, no, she didn't want a day in bed. She could do that in Malsum Pass. This vacation was her adventure, and the days were passing far too quickly already. Before she knew it, she'd be back on a plane and back to business as usual for at least another year. Three hundred sixty-five days of the same old Ginny, same old life. Gritting her teeth against the pain, Ginny pushed herself up off of the mattress. Within moments, Scott was beside her, picking her up, and cradling her in his arms.

"In case you didn't know it," he said as he carried her into the bathroom and straight into the shower. "This hotel has an amazing spa. They even offer couples massage."

A spa day? Ginny was sold.

Chapter Seven

"You know, not all adventures have to be physically challenging," Scott drawled lazily beside her as they lounged in one of the hotel pools. This one even had a bar – right *in* the pool!

She had to agree that this type of relaxation did have some merit. Especially after being worked over by a masseuse until every muscle in her body felt loose. She'd also indulged herself with a few other treatments. Some, like the steam room, had felt more like punishment – she wasn't a fan – while others had left her skin feeling amazing. Whether she had the healthy glow they promised was anyone's guess since it wasn't immediately apparent when she looked in a mirror, but her skin felt softer than ever. She'd even thrust her arm at Scott once he'd emerged from the sauna with the demand that he "Touch it".

That order had led to Scott grasping her hips with both hands and crowding her back against a wall with a mischievous twinkle in his eyes. "That's one invitation I'll never pass up," he growled into her neck as he nuzzled in close. She could feel the heat of his hands gripping her even through the fluffy white robe emblazoned with the spa logo, and Ginny's belly had clenched with anticipation, was clenching even now just thinking about it...

"Sometimes, the best experiences are the ones that don't necessarily get your blood pumping, but leave you disbelieving your eyes," Scott continued.

Ginny took a sip of her water which was loaded with slices of cucumber and sprigs of mint. According to her masseuse, the concoction was recommended after her massage and was supposed to be rejuvenating. At first, she hadn't been sure she'd be able to drink it, that first taste hitting her tongue oddly, but after a few sips, she was getting used to it. Letting her head loll lazily to the side, she looked over the top of her sunglasses at him. "Did you have something particular in mind?"

Scott grinned. "I don't want to spoil the surprise, but there's a cruise tonight that I think you'll love."

That surprise that he didn't want to spoil took Ginny's breath away as she sat in the boat with Scott's arms around her that night. The water in the lagoon they were sailing near was glowing. A bright blue illumination, and not due to any man-made lights set below the water's surface. No, this was completely natural and absolutely amazing.

"What causes it?" Ginny asked, leaning her head against Scott's shoulder.

"Microorganisms that live in the water," Scott replied against the top of her head. "But I imagine once upon a time people thought it was magic."

Ginny grinned. "Magic is much more romantic."

Scott chuckled and Ginny turned in his arms to cup his cheek. "Thank you for this. I'm afraid I got a bit carried away yesterday after climbing the cliff. I got so obsessed with ticking off even more points on my list, that I forgot I should also be *seeing* and experiencing, not just doing."

"I should be thanking you," Scott murmured as he kissed her forehead and then her nose before he dropped a quick kiss on her lip. "It's nice to see the island through your eyes. It's like I'm seeing it all again for the first time."

Sighing, he wrapped his arms around her a bit tighter and settled his head on her shoulder to nuzzle her neck. "I've been here for close to a year now, almost time to move on."

"Where are you thinking of going next?"

She felt Scott shrug but there was a hint of something she couldn't place underlying his words as he said, "I'm thinking I may return to the States. Not sure yet."

Ginny nearly bit holes in her tongue to keep from blurting out that he should come home with her to Vermont. She wouldn't ruin this idyllic bubble she found herself in by putting him on the spot or leaving herself open to that kind of rejection. Scott was on his own adventure to see the world and all the beauty it held. Yet again she had to remind herself that he wasn't a permanent fixture in her life. Scott Sloane was part of her adventure – temporary – a chapter in her story. A great chapter, yes, and one she'd revisit often in her memories she was sure, but she couldn't make this into some happily ever after fairytale. When she left this island and returned to the real world, they would both be moving on. Her to go back to Malsum Pass and her little accounting firm, him to his next destination, wherever that might be. The thought made her chest feel tight as if she wasn't able to draw air fully into her lungs, but maybe they could keep in touch. After all, in this technological age, miles meant very little... Or would that just be opening herself up for heartache? Maybe it was best to cut all ties in a clean break when her vacation was over and she bid him goodbye.

Letting out a little sigh, Ginny looked once more to the glowing waters that for some reason, no longer looked quite as bright.

By the time the boat docked, Ginny had managed to shake off her depression and was smiling again as she and Scott walked hand in hand, barefoot down the beach. In the glow cast by the nearby hotels, and aided by their keen night vision, they were able to watch the crabs skittering over the sand. Ginny found it a bit creepy, the creatures too spiderlike in her opinion, and she couldn't hold back her shudder. Feeling it, Scott wrapped his arm around her and pulled her close. "Cold? I was going to suggest ice cream, but..."

"Ice cream sounds perfect."

The next morning, Ginny was able to get out of bed much easier. A good thing too, considering she was determined to take that bike tour of the island. As with the rock climbing, her muscles were probably going to be protesting the next day, but the tour was fun and not as strenuous as climbing a cliff since the majority was downhill. And once they returned, Scott took her to visit some of the shops where locals were selling an assortment of goods. Though *shops* may not have been the best word. The area was more like a bazaar, with tables of merchandise just set up right on the street for tourists to browse, while the sellers loudly called out for attention.

Fresh produce, colorful clothing, jewelry, and even wood carvings. It was as she was examining a carving of a wolf done in exquisite detail that Scott growled in her ear, "I want to see your wolf."

Ginny swallowed hard at the intimate request and set the carving back on the table before she accidentally dropped it. "Tonight, in the hotel room," she whispered, suddenly eager to return. Her wolf was beautiful, and that wasn't conceit but fact. Her fur was a stunning coppery color that was slightly darker on her back, graduating by degrees to a lighter shade on her underbelly and legs. She wanted Scott to see her that way, but more, she wanted to see him. Several times, she'd sensed his wolf close to the surface, and had seen him in Scott's eyes, but there was nothing that compared to the up close and personal of shifting together.

Scott shook his head. "I want to run with you."

Ginny's brow scrunched in confusion. "We can't. Someone would see."

Again, he shook his head, a sly smile tilting his lips slightly. "I know a place. We'll be safe, and we can run all day." He dropped a suckling kiss to the side of her throat. "Tomorrow."

Ginny felt a twinge of trepidation. She'd never shifted to her wolf form anywhere but Malsum Pass. Within those borders, she knew she was safe, the terrain familiar, with no hidden dangers. But she trusted Scott, and her excitement of running beside him, exploring and discovering someplace new overruled any fear. It would be another adventure.

CHAPTER EIGHT

HER NERVOUSNESS RETURNED THE next day as they made the rather long trip to Scott's so-called safe place. They were heading deep into a forested section and had already passed numerous 'No Trespassing' signs. That, paired with the mist hovering just above the ground gave the area an ominous feel that only added to her misgivings. As if sensing her rising anxiety, Scott reached over and gave her hand an encouraging squeeze. "No tourists are allowed on this section of the island. It's strictly shifter domain, and any non-shifters will be quickly turned back."

Curious, Ginny looked more closely at the passing scenery as the vehicle bounced slowly over the rutted dirt path. "I didn't realize there were any shifters on the island – aside from you and me of course."

"The nest keeps pretty much to themselves, but they're native to the island."

Nest? Ginny was familiar with packs, prides, and even clans, but she'd never heard of any shifters that lived in nests. "Are they birds?" She'd heard that some large predator bird shifters – eagles, hawks, even vultures – existed, though she'd never met one personally.

"Not birds."

Ginny's lips twisted with frustration. "Okay, Mister Mysterious. Give. What kind of shifters are we talking about here?"

Scott shot her a sheepish look. "The Boas are really nice. I promise you'll like them and we'll be able to shift and run for miles in complete safety."

Ginny closed her eyes for a moment and tried not to shudder. "Please tell me that Boa is the alpha's family name and not the species."

"They would never hurt you – or anyone – it's not their way. That's why they keep to themselves."

The shudder broke loose. Snakes. And not just any snakes, but shifter snakes, so, like all shifters, they were bound to be bigger than their animal counterparts in the wild. The movie *Anaconda* flashed through her mind and she was suddenly envisioning a monstrous beast wrapped around her as it crushed her bones to powder.

Scott squeezed her hand again and held on tight. "I would never put you in danger, Ginny. You know that, right?"

Taking a deep breath, Ginny nodded. She trusted Scott, and he was right, she did know that he would never purposely endanger her but… "Just, don't leave me, okay?"

Pulling their joined hands to his lips, he kissed her knuckles. "Nothing could pry me away."

Taking strength from that declaration, Ginny prepared herself to meet the Boas.

When they walked hand in hand into the little village, Scott was once again greeted with happy shouts of "Sarge!" and Ginny felt the calming effects of such a boisterous welcome. Unfortunately, it didn't last. The male that approached them – probably the alpha or whatever the snake equivalent was called – was a big guy. Like really big. Tall, and muscular, his skin incredibly dark, but that wasn't what caused Ginny's dismay. His eyes were a light gray and his pupils were contracted to slits exactly like the creature that lived within that big body. His face was also tattooed across his cheekbones and up over his temples with greenish-gold in a crisscrossing diamond pattern… or was it a tattoo? Was his snake so close to the surface that the animal's scales were bleeding through?

"Ginny, this is Delroy."

Delroy's rather disturbing eyes moved over Ginny for a moment before he nodded and his serious countenance morphed into a grin that displayed a set of even, bright white teeth. "She's too pretty for you."

Scott chuckled, shaking his head. "So I've been told."

Ginny couldn't help but smile, as the tension seeped out of muscles she hadn't realized had been clenched in readiness to bolt.

"Go! Shift! Run!" Delroy bellowed as he turned away, his arms thrown over his head. "Tonight, we feast!"

Looking around at the wide expanse of forest, Ginny was suddenly eager to shed her clothes and shift. How long had it been since her last run? Too long. Her wolf was practically pushing against her skin to be free and Ginny was more than happy to accommodate her.

Her first sight of Scott in his wolf form took her breath away. He was beautiful. Large, robust, and healthy, his dark gray fur was thick and gleaming, while the white on his neck and underbelly shone brightly. Immediately, he stepped forward to nuzzle his nose against her neck before he licked her face. For a few moments, they pranced around each other, showing off, each admiring the other, and then they were off.

The landscape was nothing like Malsum Pass. The scents were all new and different, the feeling of the ground beneath her paws, alien, and the ever-present mist quickly dampened her coat. They ran side by side, releasing the pent-up energy of their wolves. They explored, sniffed, rolled, and even frolicked through the fragrant, tropical bush. The Boas remained within sight; their large dark bodies hanging from fruit trees or slithering through the flowering shrubs, but nothing, not even the presence of some very large snakes, could diminish Ginny's excitement at running with Scott.

They ran until they were both exhausted, yet somehow refreshed at the same time. Happiness. Ginny might even say utter bliss. She had spent this vacation stockpiling memories – the sights, the scents, the sounds, all the new experiences – but this, this would be the memory she knew she would remember the clearest and the longest. Running with Scott. Together. Their wolves free.

They were all gathered outside, seated around a long table sharing roasted chicken and fresh fruits native to this part of the island as a roaring bonfire lit the night and sent orange sparks shooting into the sky. Scott once more found that he couldn't take his eyes off of Ginny as she laughed at something one of the Boas had said. The way the light of the fire made her skin glow with radiance. Her earlier nervousness was completely forgotten, her posture re-laxed and at ease, as stories were shared, everyone piling on to the conversation with good-natured ribbing until the atmosphere was quite festive. He heard little of it, his senses completely absorbed in the grinning woman by his side.

He'd thought her beautiful from the moment he'd first laid eyes on her, but here, tonight, she *owned* him. Running with her by his side today had been a joy, so unbelievably natural and also like a puzzle piece that had always been missing had finally fallen into place allowing him to see the full picture at last. If he had any remaining sliver of doubt before, it was now gone. He was in love with Ginny Weller. He felt the knowledge singing in his blood with every beat of his heart. It hummed through his veins and reverberated through his bones.

When he'd brought up potentially moving back to the States, hinting in the hopes she'd offer an invitation, he'd sensed her hesitation. It had frustrated him, but he'd understood. She was still thinking of things as temporary. There was nothing temporary about this. She was his. He was hers. Always. When she left, he'd follow. Once she was in her home territory, he'd continue the courtship, prove to her that he was a worthy mate, worthy of her love, worthy of forever.

This bond between them was real, he felt the connection deep inside. Strong, unbreakable, permanent.

Another round of boisterous laughter and Ginny turned to look at him, her face lit by the flames and her eyes sparkling with mirth as she took his hand and laced her fingers through his. The desire to declare his love was on the tip of his tongue, but he bit it back. If she wasn't ready…

Hiding the twinge of pain that thought caused behind a smile, Scott attempted to focus on the stories being told but his brain refused to follow, instead, it was working on a plan, compiling a list. Ginny would like that, he thought, a smile of genuine amusement quirking his lips. His woman loved lists.

Chapter Nine

Her vacation had gone far too quickly. Packing in preparation for her departure, Ginny couldn't keep her mind focused on her list. Was her boarding pass ready? Did she have her passport? Who cares? She didn't. And for a woman who was so in love with lists, the thought was disconcerting. She didn't have to wonder what was wrong with her. Collapsing on the bed with a defeated breath, she snatched up her phone and scrolled through pictures. The photo she'd taken of herself on that first day in her coral bikini – that was now only a pair of bottoms that she should probably throw away. A day when she had still been naïve enough to believe that she could have an adventure and leave here better for it. But that had been before she'd met Scott Sloane.

Her chest squeezed tight and she felt a telltale prickle of tears behind her eyes as her thumb continued to flip through the images. Her with the stylist, both of them grinning at how fabulous she'd turned out for her dinner date with Scott. All the bright, smiling faces at Alvita's. Her and Scott grinning into the camera before they went snorkeling and discovered man-eating fish… Sniffing, Ginny wiped a tear from her cheek as she chuckled and continued to scroll. There were several images of her and Scott in harnesses and helmets, triumphant at the top of that cliff with the view of the island behind them, followed by images of them in matching spa robes.

Tracing her fingers over Scott's smiling features, Ginny felt more hot liquid leak down her cheek and expelled a hard breath. This was so much harder than she thought it would be. All her reminders that this was temporary hadn't done a damn lick of good. She'd fallen in love, and when she got on that plane, she'd be leaving her heart behind.

Ginny growled. She needed to stop this, she scolded herself firmly. She was acting like she was in mourning and she hadn't even left yet. She may have less than twenty-four hours before she needed to board her plane, but sitting here crying while the minutes ticked by was ridiculous. Better to spend what time was left doing something productive, something fun. Another memory to take home with her.

Swiping quickly at her face with the backs of her hands, Ginny got back to the business of packing everything except what she would need to get ready in the morning. She was supposed to meet Scott for lunch in less than an hour and the last thing she wanted was for him to see her all puffy-eyed and weepy. He'd ask her about it and what could she say? That she'd fallen in love with him? That she wanted him to choose her over his life-long dream of seeing the world? She wouldn't do that to him.

He'd left her that morning, waking her with a quick kiss to tell her that he had to take care of a few things but would meet up with her at the hotel restaurant. And when she met him, she was determined to be bright-eyed and happy.

So what did she want to do today? How did she want to spend her last day here on this amazing island? The last day of her forties? Surprisingly – or maybe not so surprising when she thought about it – the only thing that came to mind was spending her last hours with Scott. It didn't matter how, or where, or what, as long as she was with him.

Scott was all smiles when they met up just outside the entrance to the restaurant, and Ginny did her best to look cheerful but just the sight of him made her heart crack open just a little more. He wasn't fooled. Pulling her close, he tipped her chin up with a gentle finger, his smile dropping to a concerned frown. "What's wrong?"

Exactly the question she'd hoped to avoid.

Ginny shrugged. "Just a bit depressed that I leave tomorrow. Head back to reality."

Squeezing her in a hard hug, he kissed the top of her head. "We still have today."

Nodding against his shoulder, she breathed in deep, needing to hold onto his scent and commit it to memory.

As they ate a light lunch, Scott mentioned a rafting tour for her last day that he thought she'd enjoy. "Nothing strenuous," he remarked. "So you won't be sore on the plane tomorrow. But really pretty."

Ginny was game. She'd always loved rafting and kayaking but didn't do it nearly enough. Just the thought lifted her spirits, though she grew a bit nervous at her first sight of the raft. She had expected a heavy-duty inflatable raft, akin to the ones she'd ridden back in the days when she'd joined Jimmy on one of his white water rafting expeditions. What was awaiting them when they arrived was something that looked more like what Tom Hanks strapped together in the movie *Castaway* to make his escape. Completely constructed of bamboo, the raft was flat, without outer walls to keep water from spilling over, and held a raised cushioned seat that could accommodate two people, while the captain – driver – whatever he was called, stood at the front with a pole to steer them through the water.

Staring dubiously at the setup, Ginny hesitated, which got Scott chuckling. "I guarantee it's perfectly safe. These waters are calm."

Stepping aboard with the assistance of both Scott behind her and the driver in front of her, Ginny sat down and cuddled close to Scott as soon as he joined her. And once again, Scott hadn't steered her wrong. The sights from this waterway were all new and beautiful, the feel and sound of the water beneath them were calming, and the scents of the lush vegetation growing on the banks were rich and aromatic, while Scott's arm around her was a balm for her misery. It didn't take long before she was smiling, and snapping pictures as their driver pointed out various points of interest. How many of these wondrous sights would she have missed if she hadn't met Scott that first day? Too many. Because of him, her vacation had truly become an adventure. Kissing his cheek, she squeezed his hand. "Thank you."

Scott cupped her cheek, his thumb stroking gently over her skin as he gave her a soft smile. "You're welcome."

Later, at Ginny's request, she and Scott returned once more to Alvita's for dinner. She'd felt the need to say goodbye to some of the new friends she'd made on this journey. They ate, they laughed, they danced, and somehow, Ginny managed to keep the tears at bay until they returned to her hotel room. But once they were behind closed doors, the dam holding back her emotions broke and Scott held her the entire time she cried. Amazingly, she somehow managed not to beg him to come home with her. Not making him choose between her and his dreams was the right thing to do. At the moment, though, knowing it was the right thing was little consolation.

Ginny's passion took over when the tears finally dried. She needed to feel Scott inside of her, to satisfy this hunger, glut herself on his lovemaking enough so that the memories would survive a lifetime.

She practically tore at his clothes, needing the skin to skin contact, and Scott met her demand with equal fervor. It was an explosion of passion. She wouldn't have been surprised if fireworks had gone off, things got so heated. Both of them knew that their time together was coming to an end and that knowledge lent a certain desperation to their lovemaking, a need to fit a lifetime into the meager few hours that remained.

And when Scott slid inside her welcoming heat, it felt so incredibly right, that Ginny's orgasm was near-instantaneous. *This was how it should be*, her passion-dazed mind whispered, *and this is how it could always be if you just tell him how you feel...*

It was on the tip of her tongue as Ginny held Scott's body against her own in the aftermath. The 'I love you' rose effortlessly to her lips, and yet, she couldn't set the words free. Scott was far too honorable and she was afraid that if she told him she loved him, he'd sacrifice his own happiness in favor of hers. If that happened, they'd both end up miserable. Any love between them would wither under the weight of regret.

The very thought made her chest ache. So, Ginny made her decision. She would bid Scott goodbye at the airport with a hug, a kiss, and a heartfelt 'thank you.' He had made this vacation unbelievably memorable, and while she knew in her heart she would always love him, would mourn his loss, and what might have been, she *would* let him go.

Chapter Ten

THE PHONE RINGING STARTLED Ginny from a deep sleep. Groggily, she stared at her cell dancing its way across the nightstand as it vibrated until the fog in her brain cleared. She'd set like five alarms to make sure she didn't miss her flight. This one was only the first. Reaching for the phone to halt the noise, Ginny looked toward Scott's side of the bed. He wasn't there and disappointment hit her hard. He'd left without saying goodbye? Could she blame him though after she'd turned into a watering pot the night before and bawled all over him? And not dainty tears gently seeping from her eyes, but a messy, ugly cry.

Yes, actually, it turned out she could blame him. What the hell? They may not have known each other long, but she *did* know him and this desertion was completely out of character.

Sitting up, Ginny ran a hand through the tangled mess of her hair. Though maybe this was for the best, she thought with a determined nod. Yes, a clean break, no tearful goodbyes, no pathetic last-minute begging... So she'd have to take a cab to the airport like every other tourist, no big deal. No. Big. Deal.

Okay, it was a big deal, dammit.

Hearing the click of the door lock disengaging, Ginny's heart leaped into her throat. The sight of Scott walking through that door made her breathe an audible sigh of relief. They weren't over yet. Not yet... and her heart held onto that fact a little too hard.

He was grinning as he approached, his hands behind his back. "Good morning, birthday girl."

Ginny blinked. She had forgotten it was her birthday, but Scott hadn't. A sweet, melting warmth unfurled in her belly as he revealed what he'd been hiding. In one hand he held a pink box that was about half the size of a shoebox while in the other hand, he held a slightly smaller box wrapped in colorful paper with a little bow on top. Feeling tears prickle dangerously close to the surface once more, Ginny swallowed hard and attempted to will them away. She refused to cry all over this poor male again.

Sitting beside her on the bed, Scott kissed her cheek as he laid the present on her lap and opened the pink box to reveal a single cupcake thickly frosted with white icing. "Happy birthday."

Ginny inhaled and let out a groan. Chocolate with cream cheese frosting – her favorite. How had he known?

"I'd sing, but I think that could be construed as cruel and unusual punishment."

Ginny chuckled and accepted the sweet. Peeling the wax paper from the bottom, she took a bite and let out another groan, this one louder, as she licked the frosting from her lips. Holding it out to Scott, she swallowed and said, "Bite?"

Scott was staring at her lips with rapt attention, his eyes rimmed with the amber of his wolf. "I think I'd rather watch you eat," he growled.

With a devilish smile, she took a bite, and playfully let out another exaggerated groan of pleasure. A lick of her lips for his benefit and she was suddenly bursting into giggles as Scott tackled her to the mattress, her cupcake forgotten in favor of a different hunger.

"Tease," he murmured as he nuzzled her neck.

Ginny let her free hand wander down to squeeze Scott's butt. "I think we have time for a quickie."

Quickie was one word for it. Heart-pounding, glorious, and amazing, were just a few others that came to mind. In seemingly record time, Scott brought her to a shattering climax. In the short time they'd known each other, he'd learned her body in exquisite detail and every spot that made it sing. All those little places that made her squirm with need, and scream in pleasure. She had to restrain the urge to thank him for being so good in bed because that would be weird, right?

Ginny didn't remember to open her birthday present until after she'd showered and dressed, and what the paper had hidden, had brought the tears dangerously close to the surface once more. Scott had remembered how much she'd liked that little wooden wolf carved in such detail and had gone back for it – for her.

"Thank you," she choked out around the lump in her throat.

With a fond smile, Scott pulled her close and kissed her forehead. "Just a little something to remember the island."

Just a little something to remember him, she added silently. Not that she would ever forget.

She did better with the goodbyes than she thought she would. Only one tear had managed to escape as she'd hugged Scott just outside of the security checkpoint at the airport. And he'd stood there for several minutes watching her as she moved through the line before he'd raised his hand in a final farewell. That last image, she was sure, was now permanently burned into her brain.

Now, as she sat in her seat on the plane, staring out the tiny window and seeing nothing, the tears leaked out more freely as passengers stowed their gear and took their seats. She had wanted to tell him she loved him so badly that it hurt, but she had somehow managed to swallow the declaration. So much for being a mature, sophisticated female who could handle a no-strings-attached affair. A week. One week was all it took for her to fall head-over-heels in love.

Someone settled into the seat next to her, and Ginny crammed herself closer to the window. Whoever he was, he smelled strongly of cologne and scotch. Normally, she would have struck up a conversation, or at least said hello, but right now, she couldn't muster the energy.

What was Scott doing right now? Was he feeling her loss as keenly as she was feeling his or was he back to business as usual? Maybe he was planning his next adventure by throwing a dart at a map.

"Would you mind swapping seats with me?"

Ginny's head jerked up at that familiar voice. Scott was on the plane! Her inner wolf was jumping up and down with excitement. Wait – why was Scott on the plane?

Glancing her way, Scott winked at her before turning his attention back to Mr. Cologne And Scotch. The guy wasn't budging from his seat, and Scott let out a long, drawn-out sigh before he said, "Fine, I'll just say what I need to say right here."

Scott dropped his duffel at his feet, braced one hand on the overhead compartment, and leaned in to pin Ginny with a look. Her heart clenched and she leaned toward him as well, crowding her neighbor, eager to hear whatever it was Scott wanted to say.

"Ginny Weller from Vermont, I love you."

Oh, my God! Oh, my God! Oh, my God! She was going to faint. No, she wasn't. No way would she miss this...

"I've never felt this connection to any other person. This is right." Gesturing between his body and hers with a hand that nearly smacked her neighbor who was gawking up at Scott he continued, "We're right together. You're my final destination as far as I'm concerned, and I'd be a fool to just let the love of my life fly away."

The love of his life. Her jumping inner wolf began dancing the cha-cha. Her neighbor, meanwhile, finally decided to heft his bulk out of the seat, and Scott pulled back enough to allow him through. As soon as the man had passed, he leaned back in. "I want to see where this thing between us leads. How about you?"

Her heart bloomed with hope, but Ginny bit her lip. She needed to ask. "What about your dream of seeing the world, experiencing all the cultures?"

"I've seen a big chunk of this world already, and nothing compares to having someone by your side, someone you love to share it with."

"I work a lot," she cautioned and Scott waved off whatever else she was going to say.

"Maybe my next adventures will be the occasional weekend road trips exploring nearby wonders with my mate. And maybe, a week or two a year of vacation will make me appreciate the wonders I'm seeing even more. What I know, is you're my greatest adventure, Ginny. You make me want to set down roots and see what grows."

Oh, her heart...

Leaping from her seat, Ginny threw her arms around Scott to the accompaniment of applause and cheers from neighboring passengers not even trying to hide their avid curiosity. "I love you!" Ginny shouted through a mixture of laughter and tears. It felt so good to finally say it she had to say it again. "I love you so much."

Scott let out a whoop and still holding Ginny tight to his side he turned to the crowd to announce, "Did you hear that? She loves me!"

Best birthday ever.

I hope you enjoyed Fifty, Furred, and Fabulous! For more books by Kimberly Forrest, be sure to check her website https://kimberlyf orrest.com

About the Author

Kimberly Forrest is an award-winning paranormal romance author with over twenty books currently published, and more on the way. Fast-paced, steamy, and with all the feels, her books blend humor with a hint of darkness in a world where shifters, vampires, and witches exist.

An avid reader and movie buff, Kimberly makes her home in Virginia with her family and her two extremely spoiled cats.

You can contact Kimberly on her website https://kimberlyforrest.com and while you're there, sign up for her newsletter to receive some free goodies and keep up with the latest news.

You can also follow Kimberly on social media:

amazon.com/author/kimberly-forrest

www.facebook.com/kimberlyforrestauthor

https://twitter.com/KForrestAuthor

www.instagram.com/kimberlyforrestauthor

www.goodreads.com/author/show/7979880.Kimberly_Forrest

www.bookbub.com/authors/kimberly-forrest

Also by Kimberly Forrest

Christmas on Dragonback Mountain

Love and Dragons

<u>Hired Hunters Series</u>

A Hunter Born

A Hunter Turned

A Hunter Found

A Hunter Cursed

<u>Misfits & Rogues Series</u>

Tea With Monsters

Dinner with The Wolf

Chocolates from A Vampire

Brunch with An Angel

<u>The Malsum Pass Series</u>

Malsum Pass

Until You

For Her

Meant To Be

Whole-Hearted

Small Moments

Soul Deep

Christmas in Malsum Pass

Fifty, Furred, and Fabulous!